Eric Carle
From Head to Toe

Dedicated to:
Miss Frickey, my first-grade teacher in Syracuse,
New York, who discovered and nurtured my love for
drawing pictures.
Herr Krauss, my art teacher in *Gymnasium*, high
school, in Stuttgart, Germany, who introduced me to
modern art when it was forbidden to be shown.
Professor Schneidler, who inspired me when I
studied graphic design under him at the *Akademie der
Bildenden Künste*, Stuttgart.

The author and publisher thank Dr. Marianne Torbert,
Director, The Leonard Gordon Institute for Human
Development Through Play, Temple University,
Philadelphia, Pennsylvania, for her comments.

Ann Beneduce, consulting editor.

ISBN 0-590-27443-0

12 11 10 9 8 7   9/9 0 1 2 3 4/0

Printed in the U.S.A.   08

First Scholastic paperback printing, January 1999

Eric Carle
From Head to Toe

SCHOLASTIC INC.
New York Toronto London Auckland Sydney
Mexico City New Delhi Hong Kong

I am a penguin
and I turn my head.
        Can you do it?

I can do it!

I am a giraffe
and I bend my neck.
        Can you do it?

I can do it!

I am a buffalo
and I raise my shoulders.
		Can you do it?

I can do it!

I am a monkey
and I wave my arms.
Can you do it?

I am a seal
and I clap my hands.
Can you do it?

I can do it!

I am a gorilla
and I thump my chest.
Can you do it?

I can do it!

I am a cat
and I arch my back.
Can you do it?

I can do it!

I am a crocodile
and I wriggle my hips.
Can you do it?

I am a camel
and I bend my knees.
Can you do it?

I can do it!

I am a donkey
and I kick my legs.
Can you do it?

I can do it!

I am an elephant
and I stomp my foot.
Can you do it?

I can do it!

I am I
and I wiggle my toe.
Can you do it?

I can do it! I can do it!